'BUT NO, SHE'S
ABSTRACT, IS A
BIRD

OF SOUND IN
THE AIR OF AIR
SOARING...'

FERNANDO PESSOA
Born 1888, Lisbon, Kingdom of Portugal
Died 1935, Lisbon, Portugal

This selection covers poetry written by Pessoa under four
names, each with its own associated persona and style.
Originally written in Portuguese, this selection is taken from
*Selected Poems*, translated and introduced by Jonathan Griffin
for Penguin Books in 1974, supplemented in 1982 and
published in Penguin Modern Classics in 2000.

PESSOA IN PENGUIN MODERN CLASSICS
*A Little Larger than the Entire Universe*
*The Book of Disquiet*
*Selected Poems*

**FERNANDO PESSOA**

*I Have More Souls Than One*

*Translated by Jonathan Griffin*

PENGUIN BOOKS

PENGUIN CLASSICS

UK | USA | Canada | Ireland | Australia
India | New Zealand | South Africa

Penguin Books is part of the Penguin Random House group
of companies whose addresses can be found at
global.penguinrandomhouse.com.

Penguin
Random House
UK

This selection first published 2018

008

Set in 9.85/12.75 pt Dante MT Std
Typeset by Jouve (UK), Milton Keynes
Printed and bound in Great Britain by Clays Ltd, Elcograf S.p.A.

ISBN: 978-0-241-33960-2

www.greenpenguin.co.uk

# Contents

## PESSOA AS ÁLVARO DE CAMPOS

## PESSOA AS PESSOA

PESSOA AS
ALBERTO CAEIRO

# from *The Keeper of Sheep*

I

I never kept sheep,
But it is as if I did watch over them.
My soul is like a shepherd,
Knows the wind and the sun,
And goes hand in hand with the Seasons
To follow and to listen.
All the peace of Nature without people
Comes to sit by my side.
But I remain sad like a sunset
As our imagining shows it,
When a chill falls at the far side of the valley
And you feel night has come in
Like a butterfly through a window.

But my sadness is calm
Because it is natural and right
And is what there should be in the soul
When it is thinking it exists
And the hands are picking flowers without noticing which.

At a jangle of sheep-bells
Beyond the bend of the road,

My thoughts are contented.
Only, I am sorry I know they are contented,
Because, if I did not know it,
Instead of being contented and sad,
They would be cheerful and contented.
To think is uncomfortable like walking in the rain
When the wind is rising and it looks like raining more.

I have no ambitions or wants.
To be a poet is no ambition of mine.
It is my way of staying alone.

And if I do want, sometimes,
For the sake of imagining, to be a lambkin
(Or to be the whole flock
So as to move spread out all over the hill-side,
Be many things happy at the same time),
It is only because I feel what I write at sunset,
Or when a cloud passes its hand over the light
And a silence flows across the open grass.

When I sit down to write verses,
Or, as I walk along the roads or short cuts,
Write verses on the paper that is in my thought,
I feel a shepherd's crook in my hands
And see an outline of myself
There on the hill-crest,
Listening for my flock and seeing my ideas,
Or listening for my ideas and seeing my flock,

And smiling vaguely like a man who does not understand
    what is being said
And tries to pretend he understands.


I salute all those who may read me,
Doffing my broad-brimmed hat to them
As they see me in my doorway
And the bus barely makes it to the hill-crest.
I salute them and I wish them sun,
And rain, when rain is needed,
And that their houses may have
Just below an open window
A favourite chair
Where they may sit, reading my verses.
And, as they read my verses, may they think
I am some natural thing –
For instance, the ancient tree
In whose shade, when children,
They sat down suddenly, tired of playing,
And wiped the sweat from the hot forehead
With the sleeve of the striped smock.


7


From my village I see as much as from earth one can see
    of the Universe . . .
Therefore my village is as big as any other earth
Because I am the size of what I see
And not the size of my own height . . .

In the cities life is smaller
Than here at my home upon the crest of this hill.
In the city the houses shut the view and lock it,
Hide the horizon, push our gaze far away from all the sky,
Make us small because they take away from us what our
    eyes can give us,
And make us poor because our only wealth is to see.


    13


Lightly, lightly, very lightly
A wind, a very light one, passes
And goes away, still very lightly.
And I don't know what I think
And have no wish to know.


    14


I don't bother with rhymes. It is seldom
That there are two trees equal, side by side.
I think and write as the flowers have colour
But with less perfection in my way of expressing myself
Because I lack the divine simplicity
Of being all only my outside.

I look and am moved,
I am moved as water flows when the ground is sloping,
And my poetry is natural like the rising of a wind . . .

The soap-bubbles this child
Keeps blowing from a reed
Are translucently a whole philosophy.
Bright, purposeless and transient like Nature,
Friends of the eyes like things,
They are what they are
With a rounded and aerial precision,
And no one, not even the child who is letting them loose,
Pretends that they are more than what they seem.

Some are scarcely seen in the light-filled air.
They're like the breeze, which passes and barely touches
    the flowers
And which we know is passing
Only because something gets air-borne in us
And accepts everything more lucidly.

At times, on days of flawless and exact light,
When things have all the reality they can have,
I stop and ask myself
Why even I attribute
Beauty to things.

Has a flower somehow beauty?
Is there beauty somehow in a fruit?

No: they have colour and form
And existence only.
Beauty is the name of something that does not exist
Which I give to things in exchange for the pleasure they
    give me.
It signifies nothing.
And yet why do I say of things: they are beautiful?

Yes, even I, who live only by living,
Am caught up invisibly in the lies of men
About things,
About things which simply exist.

How difficult to be just oneself and not see anything but
    the visible!

30

Should they want me to have a mysticism, right, I have one.
I'm mystical, but only with the body.
My soul is simple and does not think.

My mysticism is not to try to know.
It is to live and not think about it.

I don't know what Nature is: I sing her.
I live on the crest of a hill
In a whitewashed house that stands apart,
And this is my definition.

## 44

I wake up in the night suddenly
And my watch is occupying the whole of night.
I can't feel Nature there outside.
My room is a dark thing with walls vaguely white.
Out there, there is a calm as though nothing existed.
Only the watch continues its clatter.
And that little object of cog-wheels there on my table top
Smothers the whole existence of the earth and of the sky . . .
I almost lose myself in thinking what it may signify,
But I stop short, and feel myself smiling in the night with
   the corners of my mouth,
Since the only thing my watch symbolizes or signifies
As it fills with its littleness the enormous night
Is the curious sensation of filling the enormous night
With its littleness . . .


## 47

One wildly clear day,
The kind when you wish you had done a pile of work
Not to have to do any that day,
I caught sight, like a road ahead among trees,
Of what may be the Great Secret,
That Great Mystery the false poets speak of.

I saw that there is no Nature,
That Nature does not exist,

That there are mountains, valleys, plains,
That there are trees, flowers, grasses,
That there are streams and stones,
But that there's not a whole to which this belongs,
That any real and true connection
Is a disease of our ideas.
Nature is parts without a whole.
This perhaps is that mystery they speak of.

This was what without thought or even a pause
I realized must be the truth
Which all set out to find and do not find
And I alone, because I did not try to find it, found.

### 49

I take myself indoors and shut the window.
They bring the lamp and give me goodnight,
And my contented voice gives them goodnight.
O that my life may always be this:
The day full of sun, or soft with rain,
Or stormy as if the world were coming to an end,
The evening soft and the groups of people passing
Watched with interest from the window,
The last friendly look given to the calm of the trees,
And then, the window shut, the lamp lit,
Not reading anything, nor thinking of anything, nor sleeping,
To feel life flowing over me like a stream over its bed,
And out there a great silence like a god asleep.

## The Water Gurgles

The water gurgles in the mug I raise to my mouth . . .
'It's a cool sound' says to me someone who's not
    drinking it.
I smile. The sound is only of gurgling.
I drink the water and hear nothing with my throat.

(29.5.18)

## If, After I Die

If, after I die, they should want to write my biography,
There's nothing simpler.
I've just two dates – of my birth, and of my death.
In between the one thing and the other all the days are
    mine.

I am easy to describe.
I lived like mad.
I loved things without any sentimentality.
I never had a desire I could not fulfil, because I never went
    blind.
Even hearing was to me never more than an accompaniment
    of seeing.
I understood that things are real and all different from
    each other;
I understood it with the eyes, never with thinking.
To understand it with thinking would be to find them all
    equal.

One day I felt sleepy like a child.
I closed my eyes and slept.
And by the way, I was the only Nature poet.

PESSOA AS
RICARDO REIS

## Master, Serene

Master, serene are
All hours
We waste, if in
The wasting them,
As in a jar,
We set flowers.

There are no sorrows
Nor joys either
In our life.
So let us learn,
Thoughtlessly wise,
Not to live it,

But to flow down it,
Tranquil, serene,
Letting children
Be our teachers
And our eyes be
Filled with Nature.

On the stream's edge,
On the road-verge,
It falls right –
In always the same
Light respite
From being alive.

Time passes,
Tells us nothing.
We grow old.
Let's learn, as though
Tongue in cheek,
To watch us going.

It's not worth while
To make a gesture.
There's no resisting
The cruel god
Who devours forever
His own sons.

Let us pick flowers,
Let's dip lightly
These hands of ours
In the calm streams,
That we may learn
Calm like them.

Sunflowers ever
Eyeing the sun,
From life let's go
Tranquilly, not have
Even the remorse
Of having lived.

(12.6.14)

## Crown Me with Roses

Crown me with roses,
Crown me really
    With roses –
Roses which burn out
On a forehead burning
    So soon out!
Crown me with roses
And with fleeting leafage.
    That will do.

(12.6.14)

## Apollo's Chariot Has Rolled

Apollo's chariot has rolled onwards
Out of sight. The dust it raised
Has stayed behind, filling with subtle
    Mist the horizon.

That calm flute – it is Pan's – launching
Its clear-cut tones on the idle air
Has added sadnesses to the gracious
    Day that is dying.

Warm and golden, nubile and sad
Girl, weeder on the parched farmland,
You stay on, listening (your feet
    More and more dragging)

To the ancient flute of the god persisting
With the air a subtle breeze is swelling,
And I know you are thinking of the clear goddess
    Born of the seas,

And waves are moving there, far in,
In what your tired body is feeling
While still the flute, smiling, is weeping,
    Pallidly mourning.

(12.6.14)

## The Roses of the Gardens of Adonis

The roses of the gardens of Adonis
Are what I love, Lydia, those flitting roses
   That in the day when they are born,
     Within that day, die.

The light's for them eternal, because they
Are born with the sun born already, and sink
   Before Apollo may yet leave
     The visible course he has.

Like them, let us make of our lives *one day*, –
Voluntarily, Lydia, unknowing
   That there is night before and after
     The little that we last.

(11.7.14)

## The Gods Do Not Consent

The gods do not consent to more than life.
Let us refuse everything that might hoist us
    To breathless everlasting
    Pinnacles without flowers.
Let's simply have the science of accepting
And, as long as the blood beats in our fountains
    And the same love between us
    Does not shrivel, continue
Like window-panes, transparent to the lights
And letting the sad rain trickle down freely,
    At the hot sun just lukewarm,
    And reflecting a little.

                  (17.7.14)

## The Ancient Rhythm

The ancient rhythm which belongs to bare feet,
That rhythm of the nymphs, pattern repeated,
    When in the grove's shade
    They beat out the dance sound,
Remember, you, and do it, on the white
Shore which the sea-foam leaves dark; you, still children
    Who are not yet cured
    Of being cured, restore
Rousingly the round, while Apollo bends,
Like a high branch, the blue curve which he goldens,
    And the perennial tide
    Runs on, flowing or ebbing.

(9.8.14)

## Hate You, Christ, I Do Not

Hate you, Christ, I do not, or seek. I believe
In you as in the other gods, your elders.
　　I count you as neither more nor less
　　Then they are, merely newer.

I do hate, yes, and calmly abhor people
Who seek you above the other gods, your equals.
　　I seek you where you are, not higher
　　Than them, not lower, yourself merely.

Sad god, needed perhaps because there was
None like you: one more in the Pantheon, nothing
　　More, not purer: because the whole
　　Was complete with gods, except you.

Take care, exclusive idolater of Christ: life
Is multiple, all days different from each other,
　　And only as multiple shall we
　　Be with reality and alone.

(9.10.16)

## The Wind at Peace

The wind at peace
Is creeping softly over deserted fields.
It is as if
What is . . . grass trembles with a tremor of
Its own, rather than the wind's.
And though the mild and high clouds are
Moving, it is as if
The earth were whirling fast and they were passing,
Because of great height, slowly.
Here in this wide quiet
I could forget all –
Even the life I disrecall
Would have no lodge in what I recognize.
Their false course my days would in this way
Savour true and real.

(27.2.32)

## To Be Great, Be Entire

To be great, be entire: of what's yours nothing
    Exaggerate or exclude.
Be whole in each thing. Put all that you are
    Into the least you do.
Like that on each place the whole moon
    Shines, for she lives aloft.

(14.2.33)

## I Want

I want – unknown, and calm
Because unknown, and my own
Because calm – to fill my days
With wanting no more than them.

Those whom wealth touches – their skin
Itches with the gold rash.
Those whom fame breathes upon –
Their life tarnishes.

To those for whom happiness is
Their sun, night comes round.
But to one who hopes for nothing
All that comes is grateful.

(2.3.33)

## Legion Live in Us

Legion live in us;
I think or feel and don't know
Who it is thinking, feeling.
I am merely the place
Where thinking or feeling is.

I have more souls than one.
There are more 'I's than myself.
And still I exist
Indifferent to all.
I silence them: I speak.

The crisscross thrusts
Of what I feel or don't feel
Dispute in the I I am.
Unknown. They dictate nothing
To the I I know. I write.

(13.11.35)

PESSOA AS
ÁLVARO DE CAMPOS

## Tobacconist's

I am nothing.
Never shall be anything.
Cannot will to be anything.
This apart, I have in me all the dreams of the world.

Windows of my room,
Room of one of the millions in the world about whom
    nobody knows who he is
(And if they knew who he is, what would they know?),
You give on the mystery of a street constantly trodden by
    people,
On a street inaccessible to all thoughts,
Real, impossibly real, certain, strangerly certain,
With the mystery of the things under the stones and lives,
With death to put damp in the walls and white hair
    on men,
With Destiny to drive the car of all down the roadway of
    nothing.

I, today, am defeated, as though I knew the truth.
I, today, am lucid, as though I were just going to die
And had no longer any connection with things
Except a leave-taking, this house and this side of the street
    turning into

The line of carriages of a train, and a whistle blown for
    departure
From inside my head,
And a jolt to my nerves and a creaking of bones at
    moving off.
I, today, am perplexed, like a man who has thought and
    found and forgotten.
I, today, am divided between the loyalty I owe
To the Tobacconist's on the other side of the street, as a
    thing real outside,
And to the sensation that all is dream, as a thing real inside.

I have failed altogether.
As I have not achieved any design, perhaps it was all
    nothing.
The apprenticeship they gave me –
I've dropped from it out of the window at the back of the
    house.
I went out into the country with grand designs.
But there I met with only grass and trees,
And when there were people they were just like the rest.
I move from the window, sit down in a chair. What shall I
    think about?

What do I know of what I shall be, I who don't know
    what I am?
Be whatever I think? But I think so many things!
And there are so many people thinking of being the same
    thing of which there cannot be all that many!

Genius? At this moment
A hundred thousand brains are busy dreaming of
  themselves as geniuses like me,
And history will not mark – who knows? – even one,
And nothing but manure will be left of so many future
  conquests.
No, I don't believe in me . . .
All the lunatic asylums have in them patients with many
  many certainties!

And I, who have no certainty at all, am I more certain or
  less certain?
No, not even in me . . .
In how many garrets, and non-garrets, in the world
Are there not at this hour geniuses-in-their-own-eyes
  dreaming?
How many high and noble and lucid aspirations –
Yes, really and truly high and noble and lucid –
And who knows whether realizable? –
Will never see the light of the real sun, or reach the ears
  of people?
The world is for the person who is born to conquer it,
And not for the one who dreams he can conquer it, even
  if he be right.
I have dreamed more than Napoleon performed.
I have squeezed into a hypothetical breast more loving
  kindnesses than Christ,
I have made philosophies in secret that no Kant wrote.

But I am, and perhaps always shall be, the man of the
    garret,
Even though I don't live there;
I shall always be the *one who was not born for that*;
I shall always be the one who *had qualities*;
I shall always be the one who waited for them to open to
    him the door at the foot of a wall without a door,
And sang the balled of the Infinite in a hen-coop,
And heard the voice of God in a well with a lid.
Believe in myself? No, and in nothing.
Let Nature pour out over my ardent head
Her sunshine, her rain, the wind that touches my hair,
And the rest that may come if it will, or have to come, or
    may not.
Heart-diseased slaves of the stars,
We conquer the whole world before getting out of bed;
But we wake up and it is opaque,
We get up and it is alien,
We go out of the house and it is the entire earth
Plus the solar system and the Milky Way and the Indefinite.


(Have some chocolates, little girl;
Have some chocolates!
Look, there's no metaphysics in the world except
    chocolates.
Look, all the religions teach no more than the
    confectioner's.
Eat, dirty little girl, eat!
If I could eat chocolates with the same truth as you do!

But I think and, peeling the silver paper with its fronds
    of tin,
I leave it all lying on the floor, just as I have left life.)


But at least there remains, from the bitterness of what
    will never be,
The rapid calligraphy of these verses –
Colonnade started towards the Impossible.
But at least I dedicate to myself a contempt without tears,
Noble at least in the big gesture with which I throw
The dirty laundry I am – no list – into the course of things
And stay at home without a shirt.


(You, who console, who don't exist and therefore console,
Either Greek goddess; conceived as a statue that might be
    alive,
Or Roman matron, impossibly noble and wicked,
Or troubadours' princess, most gentle and bright vision,
Or eighteenth-century marquise, décolletée and distant,
Or celebrated cocotte of one's father's time,
Or something modern – I've no very clear idea what –,
Be any of this whatever, and, if it can inspire, let it!
My heart is an overturned bucket.
Like the people who invoke spirits invoke spirits I invoke
Myself and meet with nothing.
I go to the window and see the street with absolute clarity:
I see the shops, I see the pavements, I see the traffic passing,
I see the living creatures in clothes, their paths crossing,
I see the dogs also existing,

And all this weighs on me like a sentence to banishment,
And all this is foreign, as all is.)


I have lived, have studied, have loved, and even
    believed,
And today there is not a beggar I do not envy simply for
    not being me.
I look at each one's rags and ulcers and lying,
And I think: perhaps you never lived or studied or loved
    or believed
(Because it is possible to do the reality of all that without
    doing any of it);
Perhaps you have barely existed, like when a lizard's tail is
    cut off
And it is a tail short of its lizard squirmingly.
I have made of me what I had not the skill for,
And what I could make of me I did not make.
The fancy dress I put on was the wrong one.
They knew me at once for who I was not and I did not
    expose the lie, and lost myself.
When I tried to take off the mask,
It was stuck to my face.
When I got it off and looked at myself in the glass,
I had already grown old.
I was drunk, was trying in vain to get into the costume I
    had not taken off.
I left the mask and went to sleep in the cloakroom
Like a dog that is tolerated by the management
Because he is harmless

And here I am, on the point of writing this story to prove
    I am sublime.

Musical essence of my useless verses,
If only I could meet with you as something of my own
    doing,
Instead of staying always facing the Tobacconist's
    opposite,
Trampling underfoot consciousness of existing,
Like a carpet that a drunk stumbles over
Or a doormat the gipsies stole and was worth nothing.

But the Lord of the Tobacco Store has come to the door
    and stopped in the doorway.
I look at him with the unease of a head twisted askew
And the unease of a soul understanding askew.
He will die and I shall die.
He will leave the shop-sign, I shall leave verses.
At a certain stage the shop-sign also will die, and the
    verses also.

After a certain stage the street where the shop sign was
    will die,
And the language the verses were written in.
Later will die the revolving planet on which all this took
    place.
On other satellites of other systems something like people
Will continue making things like verses and living under
    things like shop-signs,

37

Always one thing opposite another,
Always one thing as useless as another,
Always the impossible as stupid as the real,
Always the underlying mystery as sure as the sleep of the
    surface mystery,
Always this or always some other thing or neither one
    thing nor the other.

But a man has gone into the Tobacconist's (to buy some
    tobacco?)
And plausible reality has descended suddenly over me.
I half rise energetic, convinced, human,
And resolve to write these verses in which I say the contrary.

I light a cigarette as I think of writing them
And I savour in the cigarette liberation from all thought.
I follow the smoke like a route of my own
And enjoy, for a sensitive and competent moment,
Liberation from all speculations
And awareness that metaphysics is a consequence of
    feeling out of sorts.

Then I sink into my chair
And continue smoking.
As long as Destiny concedes it, I shall continue smoking.

(If I married the daughter of my laundress
    Perhaps I would be happy.)
At this I get up from the chair. I go to the window.

The man has come out of the Tobacconist's (putting
    change into his trousers pocket?).
Ah, I know him; it's Steve, he has no metaphysics.
(The Lord of the Tobacco Store has come to the door.)
As if by some divine instinct Steve has turned and has
    seen me.
He has waved me a greeting, I have shouted to him
    *Adeus ó Estêves*, and the universe
Has rebuilt me itself without ideal or hope, and the Lord
    of the Tobacconist's has smiled.

                                (15.1.28)

## I Have a Terrible Cold

I have a terrible cold,
And everyone knows how terrible colds
Alter the whole system of the universe,
Set us against life,
And make even metaphysics sneeze.
I have wasted the whole day blowing my nose.
My head is aching vaguely.
Sad condition for a minor poet!
Today I am really and truly a minor poet.
What I was in the old days was a wish; it's gone.

Goodbye for ever, queen of the fairies!
Your wings were made of sun, and I am walking here.
I shan't get well unless I go and lie down on my bed.
I never was well except lying down on the Universe.

*Excusez un Peu* . . . What a terrible cold! . . . it's physical!
I need truth and the aspirin.

(14.3.31)

## Newton's Binomial Theory

Newton's binomial theory is as beautiful as the Venus
 of Milo.
The fact is, precious few people care.

O! O! O! O! – – – O! O! O! O! O! O!   O! O! O! – – –
  O! O! O! O! O! O! O! O!   O! O! O! O! O! O! O!

(The wind out there.)

# I Am Tired

I am tired, that is clear,
Because, at a certain stage, people have to be tired.
Of what I am tired, I don't know:
It would not serve me at all to know
Since the tiredness stays just the same.
The wound hurts as it hurts
And not in function of the cause that produced it.
Yes, I am tired,
And ever so slightly smiling
At the tiredness being only this –
In the body a wish for sleep,
In the soul a desire for not thinking
And, to crown all, a luminous transparency
Of the retrospective understanding . . .
And the one luxury of not now having hopes?
I am intelligent: that's all.
I have seen much and understood much of what I have
    seen,
And there is a certain pleasure even in the tiredness this
    brings us,
That in the end the head does still serve for something.

(24.6.35)

PESSOA AS
PESSOA

## Dom Sebastião, King of Portugal

Mad, yes, mad, because I would have greatness
Such as Fate gives to none.
No tamping down in me my sureness;
Therefore, where the sand dwells, the worn
Part of me stopped, not the enduring one.

This my madness, accept it, those who can,
Dare whatever it needs.
What, without madness, is a man
More than a beast after feeding,
A corpse adjourned, the half-alive breeding?

## As She Passes

When I am sitting at the window,
Through the panes, which the snow blurs,
I see the lovely image, hers, as
She passes . . . passes . . . passes by . . .

Over me grief has thrown its veil: –
Less a creature in this world
And one more angel in the sky.

When I am sitting at the window,
Through the panes, which the snow blurs,
I think I see the image, hers,
That's not now passing . . . not passing by . . .

(5.5.02)

## Christmas

A God's born. Others die. Reality
Has neither come nor gone: a change of Error.
Now we have another Eternity,
And always the one passed away was better.

Blind, Science is working the useless ground.
Mad, Faith is living the dream of its cult.
A new God is a word – or the mere sound.
Don't seek and don't believe: all is occult.

(? 1922)

## Harvestwoman

But no, she's abstract, is a bird
Of sound in the air of air soaring,
And her soul sings unencumbered
Because the song's what makes her sing.

(1932)

## Why, O Holy One

Why, O Holy One, did you spill your word
Over my life?
Why does my false start have to have
This crown of thorns, the truth about the world?

Formerly I was wise and had no cares,
Listened, at day's end, to the homing cows,
And the farmland was solemn and primitive.
Now that I have become the truth's slave,
The gall of having it is all I have.
I am an exile here and, dead, still live.

Cursed be the day on which I asked for knowledge!
More cursed the one that gave it – for you did!
Where now is the unconsciousness – mine, early –
Which consciousness, like a suit, keeps hid?
I know, now, almost all and am left sighing . . .
Why did you give what I asked, Holiness?
I know the truth, at last, of the real Being.
Would it had pleased God I should know less!

(1932)

## She Came Looking Elegant

She came looking elegant – speed
Without haste – with a smile too –
And I, who feel with the head,
Made – pat – the poem due.

In the poem I do not treat
Of her, girl adult, turning
The corner of that street
Which is the corner, eternal.

In the poem I treat of the sea,
Wave and grief are my matter.
Re-reading recalls for me
The hard corner – or the water.

(14.8.32)

## I See Boats Moving

I see boats moving on the sea.
    Their sails, like wings of what I see,
Bring me a vague inner desire to be
Who I was without knowing what it was.
So all recalls my home self and, because
It recalls that, what I am aches in me.

(1932)

## There Was a Moment

There was a moment
When you let
Settle on my sleeve
(More a movement
Of fatigue, I believe,
Than any thought)
Your hand. And drew it
Away. Did I
Feel it, or not?

Don't know. But remember
And still feel
A kind of memory,
Firm, corporeal,
At the place where you laid
The hand, which offered
Meaning – a kind of,
Uncomprehended –
But so softly . . .
All nothing, I know.
There are, though,
On a road of the kind
Life is, things – plenty –
Uncomprehended.

Do I know whether,
As I felt your hand
Settle into place
Upon my sleeve
And a little, a little,
In my heart,
There was not a new
Rhythm in space?

As though you,
Without meaning to,
Had touched me
Inside, to say
A kind of mystery,
Sudden, ethereal,
And not known
That it had been.

So the breeze
In the boughs says
Without knowing
An imprecise
Joyful thing.

(9.5.34)

## Should Somebody One Day

Should somebody one day knock at your door
Announcing he's an emissary of mine,
Never believe him, nor that it is I;
For to knock does not go with my vainglory,
Even at the unreal door of the sky.

But should you, naturally and without hearing
Anyone knock, come to your door, unbar it
And find somebody waiting (it appears)
To dare to knock, give it some thought. It was
My emissary and I and the retinue of my glorying
In what drives to despair and what despairs.
Unbar to who does not knock at your door!

(5.9.34)

## Soon as There are Roses

Soon as there are roses, I want no roses.
I want them only when there can't be any.
    What should I do with the things, many,
    On which, at will, any hand closes?

I never want the night except when dawn
Is making it melt into gold and azure.
    That of which my soul is unsure
    Is what I must possess, that only.

For what? . . . If I knew that, I would not form
Verses to say I don't, even now, know it.
    I have a soul that's poor and cold . . .
    Ah, with what alms shall I warm her? . . .

(7.1.35)

## There Are Diseases

There are diseases worse, yes, than diseases,
Aches that don't ache even in one's soul
And yet, that are more aching than the others.
There are dreamed anguishes that are more real
Than the ones life brings us, there are sensations
Felt only by imagining
Which are more ours than our own life is.
There's so often a thing which, not existing,
Does exist, exists lingeringly
And lingeringly is ours and us . . .
Above the cloudy green of the broad river
The white circumflexes of the gulls . . .
Above the soul the useless fluttering –
What never was, nor could be, and is everything.

Give me some more wine, because life is nothing.

(19.11.35)